The Raggedy Red Squirrel

photographs and text by
Hope Ryden

DUTTON **Lodestar Books** NEW YORK

for John

Copyright © 1992 by Hope Ryden

All rights reserved. No part of this publication may be reproduced or transmitted
in any form or by any means, electronic or mechanical, including photocopy, recording, or any
information storage and retrieval system now known or to be invented,
without permission in writing from the publisher, except by a reviewer who wishes
to quote brief passages in connection with a review written for inclusion
in a magazine, newspaper, or broadcast.

Library of Congress Cataloging-in-Publication Data

Ryden, Hope.
The raggedy red squirrel/photographs and text by Hope Ryden.—1st ed.
p. cm.
"Lodestar books"
Summary: Describes how a mother red squirrel makes a nest and cares for two
babies until they can fend for themselves.
ISBN 0-525-67400-4
1. Tamiasciurus hudsonicus—Juvenile literature.
[1. Red Squirrels. 2. Squirrels.]
I. Title. II. Title: Red squirrel.
QL737.R68R89 1992
599.32'32—dc20
91-33935
CIP
AC

Published in the United States by Lodestar Books,
an affiliate of Dutton Children's Books, a division of Penguin Books USA Inc.,
375 Hudson Street, New York, New York 10014

Published simultaneously in Canada by McClelland & Stewart, Toronto

Editor: Virginia Buckley   Designer: Richard Granald, LMD

Printed in Hong Kong by Wing King Tong Co. Ltd.

First Edition   10 9 8 7 6 5 4 3 2 1

Also by Hope Ryden

Your Cat's Wild Cousins
Wild Animals of Africa ABC
Wild Animals of America ABC

The Little Deer of the Florida Keys
Bobcat
America's Bald Eagle
The Beaver

A raggedy red squirrel traveled far looking for the right place to settle down. It had to contain a stand of spruce trees.

That's because red squirrels love to eat the tiny seeds
found in spruce cones.

The red squirrel ate other kinds of food too. In spring she fed on leaf buds.

And since leaves come
out first at the tops of trees,
she climbed to the topmost
branches to find them.
She was not a bit afraid
of high places.

One day the raggedy red squirrel spied a gray squirrel
eating an acorn.

Now, a gray squirrel is *not* the same animal as a red squirrel. It is quite another species. For one thing, it is three times bigger than a red squirrel. What's more, it has different habits. A gray squirrel would never eat spruce cones. Acorns are its favorite food.

When she first saw the big squirrel, the raggedy red squirrel was annoyed. But she was also curious. As soon as the gray squirrel left, she traveled down the tree and sampled an acorn. It was good!

She was soon interrupted,
however, by the sound
of some noisy birds feeding
from a long tube. Now what
could *they* be eating?

Of course, the raggedy red squirrel had to taste the
birds' fare . . .

. . . which, as it turned out, she liked very much. In fact, she ate it all up.

That very evening she began to build her nest in, of all places, an empty birdhouse. Up and down the tree she traveled, carrying leaves in her mouth.

These she stuffed through the round door until the
birdhouse was chock-full of them. After each trip
she remained on the stoop and arranged the nesting
material just so. She had good reason to be fussy,
for she was soon to become a mother.

Not long afterward two baby red squirrels were born inside the birdhouse. At first the raggedy red squirrel stayed home with them almost all the time. She was a devoted mother.

Whenever she felt cramped, she simply went outside and napped on the stoop. She did not like to leave her babies unattended.

She did have to go off in search of food when she got
hungry. But she tried to be quick about finding it.
One day while heading home with an acorn in her
mouth, she saw something that made her angry.

The gray squirrel was hanging onto the bird feeder. The red squirrel began to scold, "Screech, churr, squeak, squeak, chip, chip, churr." But the gray squirrel did not understand the red squirrel's language and went right on eating.

This so enraged the red squirrel that she took off after the big gray, all the while yelling at the top of her lungs, "Screech, churr, squeak, squeak, chip, chip, churr." Through the treetops the two squirrels flew.

The gray squirrel ran for fifty yards before she dared
to stop and look back. To her relief she saw that the
red squirrel had given up the chase and was returning
to the bird feeder.

Once there she proclaimed to all within earshot that the feeder belonged to her and to her alone. Of course, she didn't say this in words. What she said was, "Screech, churr, squeak, squeak, chip, chip, churr."

But the big gray squirrel had better things to do than listen to a pip-squeak red squirrel one-third her weight. That very day the big gray's babies had come out of their hollow tree nest for the first time. And that meant trouble, as the raggedy red mother was about to learn.

For upon returning to *her* babies, she discovered
that one of them had left the nest. In fact, it had
slipped off the narrow stoop and was hanging onto
the bottom of the birdhouse for dear life.

When the mother red squirrel saw that her baby was in danger of falling to the ground, she acted quickly. In one swoop she snatched the youngster, pulled it up on the stoop, and then . . .

. . . stuffed it back into the nest.

Now, while she was doing this, she failed to notice that the big gray squirrel was spying on her from the bushes.

How could she keep track of her enemy with so much going on? No sooner did she put one baby back into the nest than the other one scampered onto the birdhouse roof, which was very slippery. When the little squirrel found itself sliding, it dug in its claws and refused to move, even though the mother repeatedly called it down.

When this didn't work, the raggedy red squirrel tried to *show* the baby how to come down off the roof. Again and again she hopped up beside it, dropped onto the stoop, and entered the opening. But even after she had done this twenty-two times, the frightened baby would not let go its grip and imitate her.

There was only one thing left to try. In a sudden
move the mother squirrel grabbed her baby, hauled
it over the side of the house . . .

. . . and shoved it through the doorway.

Not long afterward the gray squirrel climbed the tree and tried to look inside the birdhouse. Whatever was she up to? Luckily, the red mother was at home and could block the door with her body until the gray squirrel headed down the tree.

Then she watched the big gray run into the woods. Now she would have to move quickly. This was no longer a safe place to keep her babies. The birdhouse roof had proved too slippery to give them safe footing. And the gray squirrel was showing much too much interest in them.

That night the red squirrel carried her two
youngsters, one at a time, to a pine tree on the
edge of her property. There she settled them into
a new nest that she had made out of grass.

In this safe, new home they could practice walking
on the rough bark of branches, which was much easier
to grip than smooth wood.

In no time at all the two little squirrels learned to balance on a branch without having to hang on with all fours. This allowed them to sit up and hold food with their front paws.

Before long they were climbing up and down the tree and exploring the forest. Usually the two babies struck out in different directions. If they happened to meet, however, they touched noses in friendly greeting.

During their first weeks out of the nest, their mother
kept a close watch on them from a nearby tree. If
she spotted a person or an animal in the area, she
made a loud racket to frighten the intruder away.
"Screech, churr, squeak, squeak, chip, chip, churr."

But every day the young squirrels wandered farther from their grass nest looking for things to eat—leaves, berries, mushrooms, and seeds. Soon they would go in search of their own living spaces, for they no longer would need their mother to watch over them.

And so the raggedy red squirrel returned to the birdhouse. In a few weeks the weather would turn cold, and she needed to put on fat to help her keep warm. Every day she ate as much as she could hold.

She also gathered a huge pile of spruce cones, enough
food to last her through winter.

One chilly evening she found an old bone to gnaw on. It contained calcium, a mineral necessary to keep her teeth healthy. Without strong teeth, she could not bite into an acorn or open a spruce cone. Without strong teeth, she would starve to death.

When the first snow began to fall, she was ready for it.

So was the gray squirrel.
She had buried thousands of
acorns, more than enough
to keep her alive until spring.

Now that the weather was
cold, the red and the gray
squirrel no longer chased
each other. They both
needed to conserve their
energy just to keep warm.

In fact, they had to rest a lot. So the red squirrel fixed
up her bed.

Then she went inside the birdhouse and made
herself cozy. She would not sleep all winter the way
some animals do. Tree squirrels don't hibernate.
But she was ready to take some long naps. After all,
hadn't she worked hard to raise her babies? Didn't
she deserve to take it easy for a while?

More About the Red Squirrel in My Yard

This book is about a tree squirrel who makes her home in a birdhouse in my yard. To say that she is a tree squirrel, however, does not tell enough about her, for in North America there are ten kinds of tree squirrels—not to mention the many different species of ground squirrels that also live here. So it is important to know that the squirrel who lives in my birdhouse is a small animal, red in color, noisy in character, and a lover of pine and spruce cones. In some parts of the country she would be called a spruce squirrel; in other places she would be known simply as a red squirrel. Scientists have given this type of squirrel the Latin name of *Tamisciuruus hudsonicus.*

In this book, you also meet another species of tree squirrel—the Eastern gray. The scientific name for this animal is *Sciurus carolinensis.* Scientific names are useful if you want to find out exactly what kind of animal you are looking at. When observing the daily behavior of a particular animal, however, I like to give it a made-up name. In this case, I call the red squirrel who lives in my birdhouse the Raggedy Red Squirrel. I named her that because her fur looked tattered. Normally, a red squirrel's coat is glossy and beautiful, but not this squirrel's. I wondered what was going on. Then I discovered the reason. She was getting into fights with the gray squirrel, who also lives in my yard. And the gray squirrel is three times bigger than she!

You may have wondered about the Raggedy Red Squirrel's mate. Why isn't he pictured in this book? Actually, I never saw him, for a red squirrel father does not take part in the rearing of his young. He lives alone in another part of the woods and only associates with other red squirrels when it is time to mate. For that matter, all adult red squirrels are loners. Even squirrel pups leave their mother's habitat as soon as they are able. Each goes its separate way in search of a private place to live.

This impulse to live alone explains, in part, why red squirrels frequently make such a racket. What they mean when they say "Screech, churr, squeak, squeak, chip, chip, churr," is "get out of my living space," or "get away from my food." Another red squirrel knows what this rattling sound means and will turn back to avoid a fight. Gray squirrels, however, do not seem to understand the message. This is not surprising, since they do not talk much among themselves except to say, "chuck, chuck, chuck," or make a kind of gagging sound. So the gray squirrel pays no attention to the warning rattle of her red cousin, and this so upsets the red squirrel that she charges after her.

Although these two kinds of squirrels eat many of the same foods (including nuts, buds, tree sap, and mushrooms), they store different items for winter. The red squirrel is especially fond of the tiny seeds found in pine and spruce cones, and so she piles hundreds of these cones in a place near her winter nest. The gray squirrel, on the other hand, cannot bite into these hard cones to get the seeds. Her jaw muscles are not strong enough. Instead she buries hundreds of acorns in secret places all over my yard. So in winter these two squirrels do not compete for food—that is, until I hang up the bird feeder.